FOR BEAUTIFUL BLACK BOYS WHO BELIEVE IN A BETTER WORLD

MICHAEL W. WATERS

Illustrated by
KEISHA MORRIS

flyaway
books

"MAY I GROW LOCS, DAD?" ASKED JEREMIAH.

"Sure," said his father.

"You still need to comb your hair every day until it gets long enough," said Mom.

"I promise I will," said Jeremiah. "I can't wait to see my new locs! Maybe next week!"

His parents chuckled.

"It will take longer than that," said Dad. "But just wait and believe. One day, it will happen."

A few days later, Jeremiah saw a picture on his dad's computer. "Who's that?" he asked. "What did he do?"

"That's Trayvon Martin," said Dad. "He was a young man walking home from the store. He didn't do anything. Still, someone hurt him, and he died." Dad shook his head. "It doesn't make sense."

Jeremiah agreed, but he didn't want to talk anymore.

One day much later, Jeremiah asked, "Dad, who is that on TV? Why is he lying in the middle of the street?"

"That's Michael Brown," said Dad. "He was eighteen years old and on his way to college. He was hurt very badly, and he died." A new image appeared on the screen. "Many people say he had his hands raised when he was shot. Those people on TV are marching to remind us."

Jeremiah didn't understand. "Why would somebody shoot someone who just has his hands in the air?"

"It doesn't make sense," Dad said. "None at all."

But Jeremiah didn't want to talk anymore.

"Did you hear that?" Jeremiah asked one evening. "It sounded like gunshots!"

"I heard it," Dad said. "I'm going to see what's going on."

"Oh, no, you aren't!" said Mom. "Call 9-1-1 and stay here with us."

Mom and Dad guided Jeremiah and his sisters, Hope and Liberty, away from the windows and into the hallway.

"Why are they shooting?" asked Jeremiah.

"I don't know, son," said Mom, "but you're safe in here."

Jeremiah didn't want to talk anymore. The family stayed in the hallway for a long time, and he and his sisters drifted off to sleep in their parents' arms.

"'We will never forget.'" Jeremiah read the words from his dad's newspaper one morning. "Forget what?"

"These people were at Bible study at Mother Emanuel A.M.E. Church in South Carolina," Dad answered. "A young man came in and studied with them, but then he started shooting. The people who died are called the Charleston Nine."

"A.M.E., just like our church! But why would anyone want to do that at church?" asked Jeremiah. "Why did he shoot them?"

"Because of the color of their skin," said Dad.

"Because they were Black? That doesn't make any sense," said Jeremiah.

"No, it does not make any sense at all," said Dad.

But Jeremiah didn't want to talk anymore.

"Where were you?" Jeremiah said when Dad came home after a long day away. "I was worried."

"I'm sorry, son," said Dad. "I was invited to speak at the rally and march for the two men killed by police officers this week, Alton Sterling and Philando Castile. But afterward, there were gunshots. It took a while to make sure everyone was okay."

"Oh no!" exclaimed Jeremiah. "I'm glad you're okay too."

"So am I," said Dad as he squeezed Jeremiah in his arms. "So am I."

"Dad, what are all
those blue ribbons for?"
said Jeremiah as the family
drove to church one Sunday.
"It looks like they're everywhere!"
    "Remember when Mom and I were downtown
and someone started shooting? Five Dallas police
officers died that day," said Dad. "It's very sad. The blue
ribbons honor them."
    Jeremiah watched the endless blue ribbons passing by.
He didn't want to talk anymore.

"Dad, what is this vigil for?" said Jeremiah one afternoon.

"What's a vigil?" asked Hope.

"Yeah, what's a vigil?" said Liberty.

"It's when people gather to remember someone who has died tragically," Mom told them. "Daddy is speaking here tonight."

"Who died now?" asked Jeremiah in a frustrated huff. "What happened?"

"A young man named Jordan Edwards," said Dad. "He was fifteen years old and riding in a car when he was shot and killed by a police officer."

"That makes no sense at all," said Jeremiah.

"You're right, son," said Dad. "You're right."

But Jeremiah didn't want to talk anymore.

In the car on the way home from the vigil, Jeremiah thought about all that he had seen and heard. He imagined Jordan, the Dallas police officers, Philando, Alton, the Charleston Nine, Michael, Trayvon, and others with names he didn't know.

Later that night, Jeremiah came into his parents' room. "Mom? Dad? I'm ready to talk."

"Okay, son," said Dad. "We're listening."

Jeremiah took a deep breath. "I'm tired of people hurting each other! I'm tired of people shooting each other! I'm tired of people killing each other! I am tired of people hating each other just because they are different or because of the color of their skin!"

"You know what?" said Dad. "We're tired of all that too."

"Is there anything we can do about it?" asked Jeremiah.

"We're trying to," said Mom. "And we believe that one day, things will change."

"That's why we vote," said Dad.

"That's why we march in the streets," said Mom.

"That's why we pray," said Dad.

"That's why we organize people in our community," said Mom.

"That's why we speak out against injustice," said Dad.

"That's why we give money to important causes," said Mom.

"That's why we write books and articles, give lectures and interviews," said Dad.

"That's why we love those around us," said Mom.

"Jeremiah, every day there are people working to make this world a better place for you and your sisters and many others. And we are working with them," said Dad.

"When we look at you and your sisters and all your friends, we have great hope for the future. We believe that your generation can work to change the world too."

Jeremiah thought about that. "It's like my hair! You told me my locs would take a long time. I just had to wait and believe. And with a little help, it happened."

His parents smiled. "Yes, it happened."

"I know I can't vote yet. But I will!" said Jeremiah. "If you let me, I can march! I already pray, and I'll keep praying. I can give some of my birthday money to someone who needs it. And when I see something wrong or if I see someone hurt or bully someone else, I can speak up and get help. I can change the world!"

"Yes, you will, son!" said Dad.

"We know you will!" said Mom.

Jeremiah lifted his head, his long locs dangling, and proclaimed, "Yes! We will!"

AUTHOR'S NOTE

When I first gazed on Jeremiah, my newborn son and our oldest child, I was certain that he was the most beautiful boy ever born. My immediate convictions were to ensure that he would never be in want and to eliminate any threat to his well-being. I also realized that his Black hue almost ensured that he would encounter threats from which I could not shield him.

I was solidly confronted by this reality a few years later. As Jeremiah played with his favorite truck, I watched my television screen in horror as I learned that Troy Anthony Davis had been executed by the state of Georgia. He had been convicted in the murder of a white police officer in 1989, but serious questions had emerged. Seven witnesses who had testified against Davis recanted their stories, and some stated that their testimonies had been coerced by police who had threatened to arrest *them* for the crime if they did not turn on Davis. Again and again, Davis had been denied his request to prove his innocence by way of a polygraph test. Despite an international outcry, Davis was executed on September 21, 2011. His final words to the family of the deceased were, "I know all of you are still convinced that I'm the person that killed your father, your son and your brother, but I am innocent." To his executioners, Davis said, "For those about to take my life, may God have mercy on your souls."

For Black men and boys in America, justice is frequently fleeting.

In a 1965 debate, writer and activist James Baldwin discussed racism's impact on adults who feel powerless to shield their children from the same discrimination they have faced. He stated, "You are thirty by now, and nothing you have done has helped you escape the trap. But what is worse is that nothing you have done, and as far as you can tell nothing you *can* do, will save your son or daughter from having the same disaster and from coming to the same end."

As a young Black father, I was challenged by Davis's experience and Baldwin's words. They conspired to speak to me. While I could not keep all threats away from my child and while I still experienced some of the racial traps my forebears dealt with, I would do all I could to make Jeremiah aware of the world while offering him the safety of my presence, a listening ear, and truthful conversations. Furthermore, I committed myself to work in any way possible to make the world better for my children while preparing them to one day do the same.

This story arises from our family's experiences during several key years of Jeremiah's childhood, based on actual events that represent only a few of those affected by gun violence and racism across America. My son's piercing and persistent questions as he has become more aware of the world have only served to further inspire our family in our anti-racism work.

For Beautiful Black Boys Who Believe in a Better World is an invitation to odyssey with Jeremiah's family in pursuit of a better world, possibly best articulated by Dr. Martin Luther King Jr., who dreamed of a world where his own Black sons and daughters would not be "judged by the color of their skin but by the content of their character." It is my sincere hope that every adult who shares this story with young people will be inspired to listen well, foster discussion, and help guide those entrusted to their care as together they conspire to make the world a better place. The hope of a better world is ultimately found in our youth. We need only help them gather the tools to lead the way.

MICHAEL W. WATERS

DISCUSSION GUIDE

In this story, author Michael W. Waters takes the reader on a journey with young Jeremiah. Much like Muhammad Ali, Jeremiah must reckon at an early age with the painful truths of racism and violence in the United States. Although he could easily turn to cynicism and despair, Jeremiah comes to believe that he can change the world for the better. Muhammad Ali said, "Service to others is the rent you pay for your room here on Earth." Muhammad believed that because we have all been gifted our lives, each of us has a responsibility to help our fellow human beings. Together, our small acts of kindness, compassion, hope, and courage can and *will* change the world.

Parents, teachers, and other trusted adults play a critical role in helping children understand the historic, structural, and ongoing implications of race, racism, and racially motivated violence. We must acknowledge that the concept of race is deeply entrenched in the structure and institutions of our country. Thus, starting a conversation on race and racism may be uncomfortable, causing us to come to terms with ugly truths and painful experiences. However, if we are to create positive social change, we must bravely face these difficult issues and the effects they have on us as a society. Although challenging, speaking about race and racism with young children presents opportunities. Children have not yet endured years of consuming racist imagery and rhetoric. They have much less to "unlearn." They are also creative, compassionate, and able to think of new and exciting solutions to combat social injustice.

This discussion guide is a tool to help adults engage young people with these issues in the classroom or at home. As you embark on this important journey, remember that these courageous conversations cannot be saved for Black History Month each February. They must be a continuous part of our dialogue and our consciousness as we seek to create a more just, equitable, and peaceful world.

PREPARING YOURSELF FOR THE CONVERSATION

"What you're thinking is what you're becoming." –Muhammad Ali

- Consult some of the many rich resources that can help guide difficult conversations. We recommend exploring "Teaching Tolerance" at www.tolerance.org.
- Take ample time to assess your comfort level, historical knowledge, and personal biases before initiating a conversation. Ask yourself: What have been my personal encounters with racism and violence? As you read this book in private, note your feelings and reactions. Take time to process and understand what emotions, experiences, and information you are bringing into your setting.
- Study your history. Understand that racism is systemic and institutionalized in American culture. Take the time to research and learn about the history of racially motivated violence in the United States. Recognize that racism is not a dated collection of unpleasant terminology from a bygone era but a simultaneously overt and covert operation still in place today.
- Honor those mentioned in this book by researching their biographies. Be ready to tell their stories. Introduce your students to each individual: Trayvon Martin, Michael Brown, Alton Sterling, Philando Castile, and Jordan Edwards; the nine members of the Mother Emanuel A.M.E. Church (Cynthia Hurd, Susie Jackson, Ethel Lance, Depayne Middleton-Doctor, Clementa C. Pinckney, Tywanza Sanders, Daniel Simmons, Sharonda Coleman-Singleton, Myra Thompson); and five Dallas police officers (Senior Cpl. Lorne Ahrens, Officer Michael Krol, Sgt. Michael Smith, Officer Brent Thompson, Officer Patricio Zamarripa).
- Ground your discussions in facts and data. Conversations around race, racism, and racial violence can quickly break down into opinion instead of fact. Do your research and have data points prepared and ready around the themes discussed in this book.

ESTABLISHING A SAFE SPACE

Before reading the story in a group setting, assess the climate. What ground rules for behavior are established? Have there been any incidents of bullying or racism in your space? Be prepared to reinforce boundaries and expectations. Here are some guidelines for creating a safe space for all challenging conversations:

- Understand that young people will come to this conversation from many different standpoints.
- Avoid singling out any person or group based on what you believe to be their lived experiences.
- Consider your own experiences with racism, violence, and trauma. What are you bringing into the space?
- Acknowledge that you likely do not know every person's personal stories of racism and violence.
- Create ground rules for discussion that reinforce respect.
- Emphasize deep listening by encouraging your group to "listen to understand," especially when others choose to share personal reflections.

- Reinforce core values of empathy and compassion.
- Do not require every person to speak during discussion.
- Create time and space for quiet, individual reflection.
- Center the thoughts and ideas of your group. Remember to not get defensive if their ideas challenge your expectations or experiences.
- Acknowledge the difficulty. Let your group know from the beginning that there may be times when the story and the conversation will become uncomfortable. Affirm their right to feel angry, confused, hurt, and sad. Discuss the best ways to express those feelings.

SPEAKING ABOUT RACE IN THE CLASSROOM

"Hating people because of their color is wrong. And it doesn't matter which color does the hating. It's just plain wrong." –Muhammad Ali

- Ask students to tell you what they know about the history of race and racism in the United States. Often, students are taught a narrative that characterizes racism as in the past, with a few racist individuals as the exception. Similarly, justice and equity are often taught as the inevitable trajectory of our country, downplaying the importance of continued racial justice work and activism.
- Explain to students that everyone has a racial identity. At times, we may think that only minority groups have a race, creating the false notion that to be white is to be without race. You may illustrate this idea by sharing how we often label some Americans with their racial identity, such as "African Americans," "Asian Americans," or "Native Americans." Yet we often simply refer to White Americans as "Americans," as if their race does not exist.
- Ask: In this story, how are people treated differently because of the color of their skin? How does racism affect Jeremiah and his family?
- Ask your students if they have heard the word *privilege*. Explain that privilege is an unearned advantage or opportunity that society gives to a group of people based on their identity. In the United States, people with white skin are often granted privilege. Ask: What other identities have privilege? Acknowledge and affirm that there are many forms of prejudice and oppression that intersect with racism, such as classism, sexism, homophobia, and religious discrimination.
- Encourage your students to understand that we cannot control the privileges with which we are born or not born, yet we can all work for a more just and equitable world where no one is treated differently because of identity.

SPEAKING ABOUT VIOLENCE IN THE CLASSROOM

"Always confront the things you fear. We are only brave when we have something to lose and we still try. We can't be brave without fear." –Muhammad Ali

- Throughout the story, the author describes Jeremiah as being upset and confused by the violence he is learning about. Ask your students to reflect on a time when they saw or heard something in the news that was upsetting or confusing. Help your students to create a list of trusted adults in their lives to whom they can speak when they hear about or experience violence.
- Note where in the story Jeremiah is frustrated or angry. Ask: Do parts of the story make you feel frustrated or angry? Acknowledge that it is normal to feel angry when we see and experience injustice, because injustice is wrong. Yet we should never use these feelings as a reason to hurt other people.
- Jeremiah's father affirms his son's feelings when he agrees that the violence they are encountering "doesn't make sense." Ask: Are there parts of the story that don't make sense to you? Clarify which incidents in the story come from real life and affirm that each act of violence is an injustice.
- Jeremiah's parents do not force him to speak about the trauma and violence he is experiencing. Yet many times throughout the story, his parents affirm his feelings and offer the opportunity to share when he is ready. When Jeremiah comes to them, they respond with "We're listening." Reflect on how you can ensure that your students know that you will be available to listen when they are ready to speak. After reading the story, allow your students the space to feel and process their emotions. Reinforce that it is normal to feel anger, frustration, confusion, and sadness.
- During your discussion, allow for periods of silent reflection. Provide your students the time and space to contemplate and process what they have learned. If you feel it is appropriate to your group, have your students silently write or draw their feelings, questions, or thoughts.

EXPLORING CHANGE-MAKING

"Impossible is just a big word thrown around by small men who find it easier to live in the world they've been given than to explore the power they have to change it. Impossible is not a fact. It's an opinion. Impossible is not a declaration. It's a dare. Impossible is potential. Impossible is temporary. Impossible is nothing." –Muhammad Ali

Jeremiah observes that he may not be old enough to vote, but there is much he can do to create change. Ask: How many of you believe that you can change the world? Invite volunteers to share how they believe they can make a difference. Explain that each of them has the power to begin making the world a better place right now. Ask: What do you need in order to change the world? Allow for several responses. Suggest that your students really need only one thing to make a difference: compassion. Explain that to show compassion means to help alleviate the pain and suffering of others.

See www.flyawaybooks.com/resources for activities about becoming change-makers.

DISCUSSING THIS BOOK AT HOME

"You don't really lose when you fight for what you believe in. You lose when you fail to fight for what you care about." –Muhammad Ali

Before reading this book with your child, have a talk about racism. Explain that some people choose to hate others because of their skin color, which can lead to unjust treatment or violence. Highlight that people being hurt or killed by another person is always sad and always wrong. Invite your child to ask questions anytime during your conversation and as you read together. Read or co-read the book, looking at the illustrations and talking about what is happening in the story. Check in often to discern how your child is feeling. Let your knowledge and experience of racial violence, gun violence, and racism, as well as your child's ideas and questions, guide the conversation. You may want to talk about some of the following:

- Ask: Have you ever seen anything on television, on the internet, or in a newspaper that was confusing or frightening? Encourage your child to always speak to you when they see or hear about a news story that is puzzling or scary.
- Ask whether your child has heard of Trayvon Martin, Michael Brown, Jordan Edwards, Philando Castile, Alton Sterling, the Charleston Nine, or the five Dallas police officers. Assess what your child knows and how they came to this knowledge. Gently correct any false information your child may have heard. Point out that Jeremiah and his parents feel confused, frustrated, and sad when they learn about these individuals. Ask: How do these incidents make you feel? Be willing to share your own feelings and thoughts with your child.
- Explain that Jeremiah shows compassion when he expresses concern about the suffering of other people. Point out times when your child has shown compassion. Brainstorm ways that your family can show compassion for others in your community.
- After you finish reading, ask for your child's thoughts, questions, and reflections. Point out that it took Jeremiah a long time before he was ready to speak to his parents about his feelings. Encourage your child to take as much time as needed to think about and reflect on the story. Reassure them that you will always be ready to listen.
- Although Jeremiah is frustrated and tired by the violence he experiences, he still believes and is hopeful that he can change the world for the better. Discuss how the two of you will help each other stay hopeful.
- Tell your child that you believe that they will help change the world. Point out that although Jeremiah is still young, there are actions he can take right away to help make change. Reread the examples Jeremiah gives: he can march, pray, give, and speak up. Ask your child what they would like to do to help make the world a better place. Make sure your child knows that you are willing to help implement their ideas.

For an expanded discussion and activity guide, visit www.flyawaybooks.com/resources.

*Guide by Erin Herbert and Darryl Young Jr.,
Department of Education Programming,
Muhammad Ali Center, Louisville, Kentucky*

www.alicenter.org

**For my beautiful Black boy, Michael Jeremiah. I love you!
Now go and change the world.**

*In memory of Jordan Edwards, Botham Shem Jean, and Atatiana Jefferson.
May you find eternal rest in the arms of God.
May we continue our pursuit of justice in your names.*
—M. W. W.

**For Daraja
—K. M.**

Flyaway Books will donate a portion of the sales proceeds for this book to Moms of Black Boys United (www.mobbunited.org) and the Botham Jean Foundation (www.bothamjeanfoundation.org).

The author extends gratitude to the Louisville Institute, the Muhammad Ali Center, and Flyaway Books for ample resources and support toward the completion of this book.

Text © 2020 Michael W. Waters
Illustrations © 2020 Keisha Morris
Guide © 2020 Muhammad Ali Center

First edition
Published by Flyaway Books
Louisville, Kentucky

20 21 22 23 24 25 26 27 28 29–10 9 8 7 6 5 4 3 2

Book design by Allison Taylor
Text set in Goldsmith

Library of Congress Cataloging-in-Publication Data is on file at the Library of Congress, Washington, DC.

ISBN: 9781947888081

PRINTED IN CHINA

Most Flyaway Books are available at special quantity discounts when purchased in bulk by corporations, organizations, and special-interest groups. For more information, please e-mail SpecialSales@flyawaybooks.com.